RIVERSIDE COUNTY

P9-DDM-912

Dear Parent:

Congratulations! Your child is taking the first steps on an exciting journey. The destination? Independent reading!

STEP INTO READING® will help your child get there. The program offers five steps to reading success. Each step includes fun stories and colorful art. There are also Step into Reading Sticker Books, Step into Reading Math Readers, Step into Reading Write-In Readers, Step into Reading Phonics Readers, and Step into Reading Phonics First Steps! Boxed Sets—a complete literacy program with something for every child.

Learning to Read, Step by Step!

Ready to Read Preschool–Kindergarten
• big type and easy words • rhyme and rhythm • picture clues
For children who know the alphabet and are eager to begin reading.

Reading with Help Preschool–Grade 1
• basic vocabulary • short sentences • simple stories
For children who recognize familiar words and sound out new words with help.

Reading on Your Own Grades 1–3
• engaging characters • easy-to-follow plots • popular topics
For children who are ready to read on their own.

Reading Paragraphs Grades 2–3
• challenging vocabulary • short paragraphs • exciting stories
For newly independent readers who read simple sentences with confidence.

Ready for Chapters Grades 2–4
• chapters • longer paragraphs • full-color art
For children who want to take the plunge into chapter books but still like colorful pictures.

STEP INTO READING® is designed to give every child a successful reading experience. The grade levels are only guides. Children can progress through the steps at their own speed, developing confidence in their reading, no matter what their grade.

Remember, a lifetime love of reading starts with a single step!

To Jameson and Michael, with big kisses—L.H.H.

To my daughter, Professor Kristen—J.M.

Text copyright © 2009 by Lori Haskins Houran
Illustrations copyright © 2009 by Joe Mathieu

Published in the United States by Random House Children's Books,
a division of Random House, Inc., New York.

Step into Reading, Random House, and the Random House colophon are registered trademarks
of Random House, Inc.

Visit us on the Web! www.stepintoreading.com

Educators and librarians, for a variety of teaching tools, visit us at
www.randomhouse.com/teachers

Library of Congress Cataloging-in-Publication Data
Houran, Lori Haskins.
Too many cats / by Lori Haskins Houran ; illustrated by Joe Mathieu. — 1st ed.
    p.   cm. — (Step into reading. Step 1)
Summary: A woman's cello playing draws all of the neighborhood cats into her yard,
where they wreak havoc before starting to make their own kind of music.
ISBN 978-0-375-85197-1 (pbk.) — ISBN 978-0-375-95197-8 (lib. bdg.)
[1. Cats—Fiction. 2. Violoncellists—Fiction. 3. Music—Fiction.] I. Mathieu, Joseph, ill. II. Title.
PZ7.H27645Too 2009
[E]—dc22   2008001576

Printed in the United States of America

10 9 8 7 6 5 4 3 2 1

First Edition

Too Many Cats

by Lori Haskins Houran
illustrated by Joe Mathieu

Random House New York

Black cat.

Gray cat.

Rich cat.

Stray cat.

Any more cats?

Many more cats!

Slinky cat.

Stinky cat.

Silly cat.

Chilly cat.

Furry cat.

Purry cat.

Hurry, hurry, hurry, cat!

Nice cat.

Mean cat.

White cat.

Green cat!

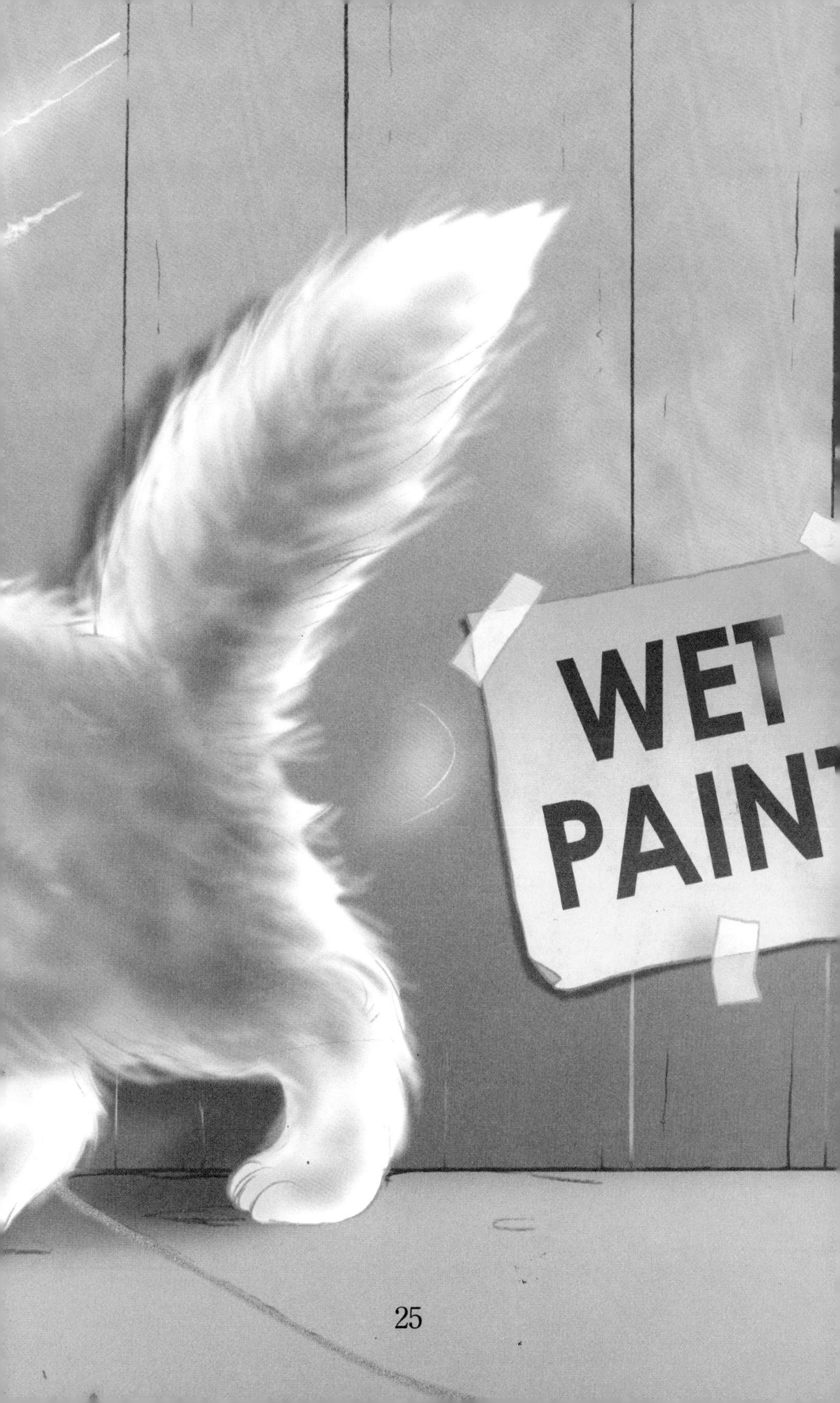
WET
PAINT

All these cats,
they like one thing.

All these cats,
they like to . . .

29

31